The Rose Horse

The Rose Horse

DEBORAH LEE ROSE

Illustrated by Greg Shed

HARCOURT BRACE & COMPANY

San Diego   New York   London

Text copyright © 1995 by Deborah Lee Rose

"*Rozhinkes mit Mandlen* (Raisins and Almonds)"
by Abraham Goldfaden, 1896, from the operetta *Shulamis*

Illustrations copyright © 1995 by Greg Shed

"MEET ME TONIGHT IN DREAMLAND"
Words by Beth Slater Whitson and Music by Leo Friedman
Copyright © 1909 by Leo Friedman. Copyright renewed and assigned to
Shapiro, Bernstein & Co., Inc. New York and Will Rossiter, Chicago, Illinois.
Published by Shapiro, Bernstein & Co., Inc. and Will Rossiter. Used By Permission.

Library of Congress Cataloging-in-Publication Data
Rose, Deborah Lee.
The rose horse/by Deborah Lee Rose; illustrated by Greg Shed—1st ed.
p. cm.
Summary: When Lily goes to Coney Island in 1909 to visit her newborn sister,
she learns about the art and traditions of the Jewish wood-carvers who
make the carousel animals there.
ISBN 0-15-200068-2
[1. Merry-go-round—Fiction. 2. Wood carving—Fiction. 3. Jews—Fiction.
4. Babies—Fiction. 5. Coney Island (New York, N.Y.)—Fiction.]
I. Title.
PZ7.R7149Ro 1996
[Fic]—dc20   94-19629

The text was set in Bulmer.
Designed by Kaelin Chappell
First edition
A B C D E
Printed in the United States of America

In memory of my father,
Bernard Rose,
whose art was a gift
—D.L.R.

To Jeannette,
with thanks for your
words of encouragement
—G.S.

CONTENTS

AUTHOR'S NOTE

Among the greatest American carousel makers of the early twentieth century were several Jewish wood-carvers. They came to the United States with two million other East European Jews who sought religious freedom and a better life.

These artists carved elaborate horses, wild animals, and mythical beasts that filled carousels across the country and helped create a new American art form. At the same time, a few carvers carried on an old European tradition, creating special pieces of art for the synagogue.

This story was inspired by their work.

The events and characters are fictional—except four real figures whose histories place them at Brooklyn's legendary Coney Island during the heyday of American carousel making. They are Charles Feltman, the immigrant entrepreneur who gave America the "red hot" or "hot dog"; Lillian Russell, the famed actress known as the American Beauty; Captain Jack Bonavita, the dashing lion tamer of Bostock's Arena; and Doctor Martin Couney, whose incubator-clinic sideshows saved the lives of thousands of premature babies.

The Rose Horse

Coney Island, 1909

A WET BREEZE crinkled Lily's nose with the strong odor of fish and salt.

"What is that smell, *Totte?*" she demanded.

"That"—her father took a deep breath—"is Coney Island."

Lily craned her neck to peer out the open trolley window.

"I have not seen the ocean since we first came to New York, *techterl*, but I remember the smell," her father said.

Lily sniffed, trying to recall the trip to America on the big boat. She had just been a baby then. Now there was a new baby, named Rose, born a week ago during *Pesach*.

"Your sister came too early," her father had told her late at night when he returned from the hospital. "The doctor said the only chance was to take her to Coney Island right away."

Without even coming home, *Momme* and the new baby had gone in the horse-drawn ambulance to a special clinic at Coney Island. Lily and her father had come all the way on the trolley to find them.

"Look!" Lily tugged at her father's sleeve. "That sign says DREAMLAND. That's where you said the incubator clinic is. We should get off!" She jumped from her seat and pulled her father to get up.

"Not yet," said her father. "First we must go to my cousin's shop and tell him we've come. Then we'll go find *Momme* and our *reyzele*."

Lily plopped back down and stared out the window. The street was full of people strolling and stopping to look at the buildings that lined Surf Avenue. WHIRLWIND RIDE! SHOOTING GALLERY! SCENIC RAILWAY! blared the signs above their heads.

At one corner Lily noticed a large crowd gathered. She could hear music and see flashing lights. Suddenly a woman's hat popped above the crowd and disappeared, followed by another and another.

"You've never seen a carousel before," said her father

as Lily stared in amazement. "My cousin makes the animals for people to ride. Soon you'll see."

A few blocks later the trolley grumbled to a stop. Lily and her father climbed off and turned down a quiet side street. At a large building with wagons lined up in front, they went in.

The room they entered smelled of hot glue and sawdust, like the furniture shop where her father worked, Lily thought.

"*Totte*," she whispered as her eyes adjusted from the brightness of the street, "they're horses!"

From one side to the other, carved wooden horses filled the room. Some stood on three legs, with one front hoof poised in midstep. Some pranced on their hind legs, with both front legs lifted high off the floor. Others jumped through the air with all four feet above the ground, held up by wooden posts. Everywhere, carved heads, bodies, and legs of horses crowded the corners.

By a window, a man in a white apron stood examining a half-carved horse's head. Lily felt her nose tickle from the sawdust in the air. Before she could stop herself, she sneezed! The man looked up, startled, then came over quickly.

"Srul," he said kindly, grasping Lily's father by the shoulders.

"Shmil, it's good to see you," said her father. "Lily, this is my cousin Samuel. We learned to carve together in Kishinev."

He rested his hand on her hair.

"This," he said, "is Lily."

"Welcome to Coney Island, Lily." Samuel grinned, shaking her hand emphatically. "You see how we need your father's help to finish all these horses! Since the fire last year, there are many figures to repair."

Samuel showed them around the shop. The walls of the room where they stood were lined with drawings of animals. Beneath, carvers sawed, noisily cutting out wood blocks of different shapes and sizes. Each figure took many such blocks, Samuel explained. They were glued together, then sanded smooth so the animal seemed to be carved from a single piece of wood.

Lily watched one carver put final touches on a horse's bridle. Carefully he tapped a blunt mallet against a sharp chisel, chipping the strap lines right into the horse's wooden jaw.

Beyond the carving room was the paint room, where Lily saw white-coated horses being dressed in silvery armor and golden tassels. There were other animals, too— a lunging tiger with orange and black stripes, a long-necked giraffe as tall as the ceiling, and a bluish green

creature with a horse's head and forelegs and the tail of a fish.

"That's a hippocampus, a magical seahorse," Samuel told her.

The third room was the showroom where the newest figures were displayed. Lily walked slowly around a lion with bared teeth and a flame red chariot pulled by smoke-breathing dragons. In the center of the room she stopped.

"What do you think?" asked Samuel proudly. "She's a palomino, the Golden Horse of the West."

Lily gazed at the figure in front of her. The horse was the color of honey with a milk white mane and tail. She was what Samuel had called a jumper, with all four feet in the air. Her mane was tousled and her mouth was wide open as if she were running at top speed. Along her bridle and around the edge of her saddle were carved garlands of flowers.

"A rose horse," said Lily, half out loud.

"This rose horse, as you call her, is going onto the carousel at Feltman's restaurant tomorrow. How would you like to be the very first rider?" asked Samuel.

Lily nodded, her eyes wide.

"That's for tomorrow, *techterl*," said her father. "Now it's time to go find our other Rose."

Dreamland

AT THE ENTRANCE to Dreamland Park, a woman selling tickets told them where to find the incubator building.

"Past Bostock's wild animal show, along the lagoon. Keep walking till you hear the spiel."

Lily's father pushed through the turnstile. Lily followed him into a huge courtyard surrounded by tall white columns and crisscrossed by a wide footbridge. Her eyes traced the bridge across the plaza to the door of a towering stone-fronted castle. Behind the castle, a snow-covered mountain glittered in the hot afternoon sun.

"Red hots! Get'cha red hots here!" yelled a boy in knee pants, pushing a wheeled cart.

Lily licked her lips at the warm, meaty smell, then ran to catch up with her father. As they walked, a troupe of acrobats tumbled past them, launching each other through the air. A train of circus ponies, some no higher than her chin, trotted by on Lily's right. Nearby, a juggler tossed a burning sword into the sky, then spun around to catch it behind his back.

Outside Bostock's Arena, the sight was even more incredible—a woman wearing a live snake around her shoulders! Lily stood mesmerized, watching the serpent coil and uncoil, until a loud roar made her jump.

"That, my friends, is Sultan, King of the Beasts!" barked a man by the door. "Step inside and see what happens when he meets the only human who can control him!"

Lily felt her father's grip tighten on her hand and his pace quicken. They hurried toward the man-made lagoon that was filled with boats gliding back and forth. From the water rose a high white tower with six golden eagles carved on the front. Lily stared up at the top, to the DREAMLAND sign she had seen from the trolley.

"This way, folks, to see the babies born too soon!" A deep voice distracted her. Just past the lagoon, Lily saw a tall, dark-haired man under a sign that read: ALL THE WORLD LOVES A BABY.

"These infants cannot see or hear you," the man told the crowd, "but you can inspect the scientific equipment that keeps them alive. Our newest arrivals are twins—less than three pounds each! Take my word for it. Don't pass the babies by!"

When the crowd moved on, Lily's father spoke to the man. He waved them inside the incubator building to a room lined with glass. Through the wall Lily could see a row of tiny cribs, a baby in each one.

"Which is Rose?" she asked.

Her father glanced around as a woman in a white uniform entered the room.

"We're looking for my sister, Rose," she blurted.

"You must be Lily, then," said the woman. "Your mother will be right out. She just finished nursing."

Lily rushed to hug her mother as she came through the nursery door.

"I wondered when you would find us," her mother said, smoothing Lily's hair.

Her mother's hand smelled of strong soap.

"They must show them to the whole world like this, Mirel?" her father said under his breath.

"The money people pay to see them buys all the

special equipment and food," her mother replied. "What Doctor Couney and the nurses do here is a miracle. Come, look."

She drew them toward the corner of the room and tapped on the glass in front of the last crib.

"Rose," she said softly, "your *totte* and Lily are here."

The tiny baby wrinkled her nose in her sleep. Lily touched the glass as her mother had done. Her sister's eyelids fluttered.

"Can I hold her?" Lily asked.

"Not yet, but you can visit her once every week until she's strong enough to leave the incubator," her mother said.

"When will that be?" asked Lily, disappointed.

"Six more weeks, the doctor says."

Her mother told them how one baby had come to the clinic wearing a *k'nehore bendl,* a red string tied on his arm for good luck. Another baby had worn a necklace with a charm made of garlic.

"Their mothers think that will keep them safe from the evil eye," she explained.

"Their mothers came, too?" Lily asked.

"No, *neshomele,* most can't travel this far, but their babies still need mother's milk. That's why I spend so much time here."

Lily's mother leaned down to kiss her cheek. "After the next nursing, I'll come and tell you more," she said.

Her mother disappeared through the nursery door. Lily waved good-bye to the wall of babies. Then she and her father retraced their steps through Dreamland and headed for Samuel's house.

Counting *the* Omer

"Six more weeks is a long time," complained Lily, scraping a curl from the fat carrot she held in her hand.

"By the end it will seem more like six days," said Golda, Samuel's wife, who had welcomed her with a hug and a pot of vegetables to cut for soup.

"How will we know when it's almost over?" Lily pressed.

Golda looked at her sideways, setting a blue-speckled teapot on the black stove.

"I almost forgot," she murmured, then said loudly, "Lily, come with me."

She led Lily up a narrow staircase to the attic, picking her way past trunks and baskets to a flat bundle wrapped in a faded quilt.

"What's that?" Lily asked.

Golda unfolded the quilt to show Lily what looked like a large book made of wood. Vines and flowers were carved all around the edges and three holes were cut from the front. Through one opening, Lily could see the number 49 and Hebrew letters written on yellow paper.

"It's an *omer* calendar," Golda said. "Your grandfather carved it for the synagogue in Kishinev."

She turned the wooden piece over. Behind the frontplate was a scroll wound on two thin wooden rods turned by brass knobs.

"What's it for?"

"For counting the *omer*."

"What does that mean?"

"It means the seven weeks we count from *Pesach,* when the Jews escaped from Egypt, to *Shevuos,* when God gave them the Torah," Golda explained.

She twisted the calendar knobs slightly.

"Your sister was born during *Pesach*. Your mother hopes she'll be home by *Shevuos*. I thought we could use this calendar to mark the rest of the weeks."

"How does it work?" Lily asked.

"I'll show you after supper. Come, I hear your mother."

They carried the calendar down the steps, Golda holding the bottom while Lily steadied the top.

During the meal, Lily's mother told them about the clinic and the babies brought to its heated incubators from every part of the city.

"Preemies, they call the babies. They're only allowed to breathe fresh air, piped in from outside the building. Below the cribs, they have hot-water coils to keep the air inside warm and wet," she said.

Some infants were so small they could not nurse and had to be fed from a tiny dropper, she continued. All the wet nurses, whose milk they drank, were forbidden to eat food from the pushcarts.

"Does that mean they all have to keep kosher?" asked Lily.

"Not quite," her mother answered. "It means they mustn't eat any foods that could make them sick or spoil their milk."

By the time they were finished, it was already dark. Lily helped clear the table and set the calendar on the clean oilcloth.

"By my count," said Golda, "tonight begins the ninth day of the *omer*—one week and two days. All right, Lily, turn the scroll until the number nine shows."

Lily twisted the knobs slowly until 9 was in place.

"Tomorrow night we'll count the tenth day, and every night after that, up to forty-nine," Golda said.

A little later Lily's mother took her into the parlor to help make up her bed on the sofa.

"It's good that you found *Zeyde*'s calendar to count the weeks we're here," she said as Lily slid between the sheets. "In Kishinev, *Totte*'s father was known for his carving."

Lily's mother turned down the gaslight and pulled Golda's wooden rocker close to the sofa.

"Where will you sleep, *Momme*?" Lily asked.

"At the clinic, so I can help feed the babies during the night," her mother answered tiredly. "*Totte* will stay here. I'll come every evening for supper. Now, do you need a song before I go, to help you fall asleep?"

" '*Rozhinkes mit Mandlen*,' *Momme*, the part where the mother sings a lullaby and the white goat is under the baby's cradle."

Her mother closed her eyes and rocked as she sang:

> "*Unter Yideles vigele*
> *Shteyt a klorvays tzigele.*
> *Dos tzigele iz geforn handlen.*
> *Dos vet zayn dayn baruf,*
> *Rozhinkes mit mandlen.*
> *Shlof zhe, Yidele, shlof.*"

"Under Yidele's little cradle
  Stands a pure white little goat.
  The little goat went trading.
  This will be your work,
  Raisins and almonds.
  So sleep then, Yidele, sleep."

The Rose Horse

JOLD ON, LILY," said her father the next morning
as he boosted her onto the saddle. Lily grabbed
the pole in front of her with both hands. All
around, people hurried to find seats on the carousel.
Next to her a girl with a sky blue hair ribbon swung herself onto a large gray cat holding a fish in its mouth.

Lily patted the rose horse with her right hand. She
could feel the carved edges of the bridle and the smooth
surface of the horse's neck. A boy in a wool cap plucked
the ticket from her fist. The band organ struck up a
waltz, and the carousel began to turn.

Lily's horse rose and fell, pulled by the brass crank overhead. From the corner of her eye, she noticed the girl with the blue ribbon let go with both hands and lean forward. Lily did the same and the breeze rushed into her face as the carousel picked up speed. Suddenly it seemed that she and the girl were racing, passing each other over and over as the horse, then the cat, climbed and sank.

Lily saw Golda wave from the booth where she stood selling tickets. Her father watched from the crowd, his arms folded tightly against his chest. Lily felt the air on her cheeks grow warmer, and realized the rose horse was slowing down. The carousel swung around one more time, and her father stepped up to help her off.

"What song were they playing, *Totte?*" she asked as they sat on a nearby bench.

"It's called the Dreamland waltz," announced a child's voice behind them.

Lily turned to see the girl with the blue hair ribbon darting away into the crowd.

The Romance Side

ALMOST EVERY DAY after that, Lily went to Felt-man's to ride the rose horse and help Golda sell tickets. Lily loved the cool morning walks along Surf Avenue before the concessions opened. By noon, when the crowds grew large, she went back to watch her father and the other carvers and help around the shop.

At first Samuel would only let her sweep up the wood chips that fell from the chisels.

"That's how all good carvers start," he teased her affectionately.

Then, after four weeks of counting the *omer,* one of the carousel painters got sick.

"The season opens next week. We can't afford to fall behind on the orders," Samuel told her father. "I think it's time Lily learned to paint."

The painting room smelled of turpentine. Lily's father tied a large apron over her clothes and showed her how to dip the brush in the white undercoat so none dripped off. She practiced making long brush strokes on an un-carved piece of wood. When she was ready she started on a stander her father had made, its right front leg lifted high and an eagle carved below the saddle.

First she painted the horse's left side. Then came the more carved right side, the "romance side," that would face the crowd as the carousel turned. She was finishing the horse's mane when Samuel came in, leading two visitors.

"This way, Mr. Feltman," he said, pointing toward the display room.

Lily stretched on tiptoe to peek over the horse's back. She could see a man in a straw boater and a woman in a white shirtwaist, a dark sea green skirt, and a broad-brimmed hat trimmed with fresh lilacs. As she moved, the woman reminded Lily of the boats on Dreamland's lagoon. The room was filled with the smell of flowers.

Too late, Lily dropped her paintbrush and clapped her hands to her mouth.

"Ah-shyoo!"

"La!" said the woman, turning around.

Lily ducked down and scrubbed her face with her apron.

"Here," said the visitor, pulling a white handkerchief from her sleeve. "This might do better."

She reached under the horse's neck. Firmly she tucked the square in Lily's hand.

"Thank you," Lily mumbled, dabbing at her nose and mouth.

"What is your name?" asked the woman.

Lily edged her way around the front of the horse's head.

"It's Lily," she answered, looking up shyly.

"Well, so is mine," said the woman, smiling. She leaned her head down toward Lily. "I picked it myself, because I loved all the *l*'s in it!"

The visitor's face was so close, Lily could see her own reflection in the woman's wide blue eyes. Suddenly she remembered the handkerchief and started to give it back.

"Oh, no," said the woman, stopping Lily's hand. "You must keep this as a gift, from one Lily to another."

She folded Lily's fingers around the silk square and squeezed them gently. Then she straightened up, hooked her arm in her companion's, and strolled from the room. Samuel winked at Lily and followed them.

"Do you know who that was?" Samuel exclaimed when he returned. "Feltman, the Hot Dog King, himself!"

"Was the lady with him a queen?" asked Lily.

"Queen of the stage," said Samuel admiringly. "Here, take another look."

He guided her to the window. Lily watched outside as the woman climbed gracefully onto a gleaming two-wheeled bicycle. The handlebars sparkled in the sun as she pedaled slowly away down the street.

"That bicycle is solid-gold plated," said Samuel. "I know because the rider is Miss Lillian Russell. She's the most famous actress in America. They call her the American Beauty. They say she even travels across the country in her own Pullman train car."

"What's she doing at Coney Island?" Lily asked.

"She's not the only famous one who comes for the ocean," Samuel replied, "and for the horse races at Brighton Beach and Sheepshead Bay."

Lily had never met anyone famous before. She lifted the silk hankerchief to her face and breathed in the faint lilac scent, imagining what faraway places she would go in her very own train car.

"*Techterl.*" Her father's voice broke into her thoughts. "Look who's here."

Lily opened her eyes. Her mother stood in the door-way.

"You've graduated to painting, Lily. No more sweeping wood chips." Her mother chuckled softly. "If you're done for now, I thought we could take a walk by the ocean. Doctor Couney says I need some time away from the clinic."

The sun was a golden fireball over the beach. Lily skipped across the hot sand and plunged her feet in the surf. The cool water foamed around her ankles and bumped something hard against them. She bent to catch it, cradling it in her palm as the salt water ran out through her fingers. It was a shell, polished smooth as a mirror.

"Momme," she asked, holding it up to her mother to see, "where did my name come from?"

"Your name?" said her mother. "Didn't I ever tell you? Your name and Rose's both come from the same place in the Bible, from King Solomon's Song of Songs."

She looked out toward the waves glistening like silver threads.

" 'I am the rose of Sharon and the lily of the valleys,' " she recited. " 'As the lily among thorns, so is my love among the daughters.' My mother used to read that to us in Kishinev during *Pesach.*"

"Do you miss her?" Lily asked.

"Yes, especially now," her mother said, sitting on the sand.

"Do you ever want to go back?"

"Only to see her, never to live."

Lily's mother turned and pointed to the far end of the beach.

"You see that lighthouse at Norton's Point? That was the first light I saw in America, even before the Statue of Liberty. The boat came past Coney Island early. I saw that light and I held you up to see. I whispered to you, 'This is America, *di Goldene Medine.*' "

She scooped up a fistful of wet sand.

"You know what you did then?" Her mother laughed. "You cried because I was holding you too tight!"

She drew back her arm and pitched the sand as far as she could into the waves. Lily followed her, the two of them tossing sand and splashing until both were drenched from neck to toe. Then together, they walked up the beach to the street, put on their shoes, and returned home.

"Quite a day," said her mother after supper, as Lily got ready for bed. "Would you like to hear *'Rozhinkes mit Mandlen'* again tonight?"

"No, *Momme,* something else. Do you know the Dreamland waltz?"

"Where did you hear that?"

"At Feltman's carousel."

"I know it," said her mother. She leaned back in the rocking chair and hummed a few notes. Then she sang:

"Meet me to-night in Dreamland,
　Under the silv'ry moon.
　Meet me to-night in Dreamland,
　Where love's sweet roses bloom.
　Come with the love light gleaming
　In your dear eyes of blue.
　Meet me in Dreamland,
　Sweet dreamy Dreamland,
　There let my dreams come true."

Lag B'Omer

ONE NIGHT the next week Lily's mother was late for supper.

"Something's wrong," her father said, jumping up again to look out the window.

"Probably a new baby came today and they needed her help," Golda suggested. "Don't worry, she'll be here soon."

Lily sat quietly, her food untouched, while her father and cousins talked of the crowds expected the next day.

"More than two hundred thousand, according to the *Brooklyn Daily Eagle*," Samuel marveled. "That would be the biggest Decoration Day turnout in Coney Island history!"

By the time they turned the *omer* calendar to 33, Lily's mother still had not come. Her father left for Dreamland to find out what had happened. Lily stayed at the table with Golda, leafing through the Sears, Roebuck catalogue while Samuel read the *Forverts*.

"Listen to this," he said, glancing up from the Yiddish newspaper. "The commissioner of immigration has decided that any immigrant who wants to make it past Ellis Island must have twenty-five dollars in his pocket! If that had been the rule when we got here, we'd all be back in Kishinev now."

Long after Samuel and Golda went to sleep, Lily sat in the rocker, watching through the parlor curtains for the red and white flashes of light from Norton's Point. She dreamed that her mother held her up to see them.

When she woke, a light burned in the kitchen. She found her father at the table, his tools spread alongside a large, uncarved piece of wood.

"Is *Momme* all right?"

"Lily! I didn't see you there. Yes, she's all right."

"What are you making?" she asked. "Another carousel horse?"

"No, a carving for the synagogue, a gift for Rose's

naming ceremony," her father replied. "We've decided to give her a Hebrew name."

"I don't have a Hebrew name," said Lily, surprised.

"Things were different when you were born."

"Is something wrong?" Lily asked, her voice tight.

Her father's fingers traced an invisible design over the wood.

"Rose is very sick, Lily, some of the other babies, too," he said. "That's why *Momme* was not here tonight."

"Is she going to die?"

"Don't even think such a thing!" Her father slammed the table with his hand.

Lily ran from the kitchen, tears burning her throat. She stumbled into the rocking chair and threw her arms over her eyes. She heard her father's footsteps brush the floor next to her.

"I want *Momme* to come back!" she sobbed.

Her father stooped down in front of her.

"She'll come as soon as she can, Lily," he said. "Listen to me."

Lily wiped her wrist across her wet cheeks.

"You remember tonight, when we counted the thirty-third day of the *omer?*" her father asked, holding both her hands. "We call that *Lag B'Omer.* A long time ago

this day marked the end of a terrible sickness. We must hope the sickness among the babies ends soon as well."

"If Rose gets better, and you give her a Hebrew name, I want one," she said, sniffing.

"Then we should think of a good one. Now, back to bed."

Lily woke early the next morning to find her father already at the kitchen table, carving. She leaned over his shoulder to see.

"What will it be?" she asked.

"A decoration for the ark where the Torah is kept," he answered wearily.

"When will you finish it?"

"I don't know yet."

"Will we go to see Rose today?"

"No!" snapped her father. "You stay away from Dreamland today."

He pushed the carving from him.

"You'd better get ready," he told her. "Golda is waiting for you."

As she left the room Lily cast a quick look at her father's work. She could just see the outline of an open book and the shapes of animals emerging from the wood.

Decoration Day

COME ON, LILY," Golda urged, hurrying along Surf Avenue.

The street was jammed with people lined up to watch the Decoration Day parade. By the time Lily reached Feltman's, the rose horse was already taken. She watched from the side as the girl with the sky blue hair ribbon sailed round and round to the Dreamland waltz. When the music stopped, the girl climbed down and stood in front of her.

"Your name's Lily, right?" she asked.

Lily nodded.

"You don't go to school around here, do you?"

"We're just here while my sister's in the incubator at Dreamland," replied Lily.

"My name's Mae," the girl said. "My father's a police sergeant. He saved four people in the fire last year. He even helped move some of those incubator babies when they thought the fire might spread to Dreamland."

Lily stared at her, wanting to hear more.

"The whole force is marching today," Mae told her. "You coming?"

Lily struggled to keep sight of Mae as they wriggled to the front of the crowd. Down Surf Avenue rolled the fire engines, pulled by dark bay horses tossing red, white, and blue bridle plumes. Next marched the police, Mae's father in the lead. Beyond, Lily could see a line of schoolchildren waving flags. Behind them came rows of soldiers, some in peaked Civil War caps, carrying rifles against their shoulders.

"C'mon!" Mae yanked Lily's arm as the procession snaked past. "I've got free tickets to Bostock's Arena."

"I can't go to Dreamland today." Lily hesitated.

"Why not?" asked Mae impatiently.

"My father . . . I don't have money for the entrance."

"Don't worry, I'll get you in," Mae assured her.

At Dreamland, Mae waved to the ticket seller and ducked under the turnstile, pulling Lily after her. The whitewashed plaza was thick with sightseers. In the background Lily and Mae could hear the shrieks of riders on the giant roller coaster.

"See what you have only dreamed of, ladies and gentlemen!" hollered a tuxedoed announcer nearby. "The Human Butterfly . . . the Electric Dairy Farm . . . headhunters . . . deep-sea divers . . . thirty shows to pick from, all new! You know what they say about Dreamland— 'Everything new but the ocean!' "

"I have a better idea," said Mae. "There's still time before the animal show. Let's go up the lagoon tower. You can see fifty miles from the top!"

"How do you get up there?" asked Lily.

"I'll show you."

The two girls ran hand in hand to the tower. By the doorway, a red-coated man stood waiting in a carpeted booth.

"Who's your friend, Mae?" he asked.

"Her name's Lily. Her sister's in one of those incubators."

"You don't say. Where's the sergeant today?"

"He's in the parade," Mae answered proudly.

"Well, let's take a look, then. Going up," the man said, his voice rising with the words.

Mae hopped into the booth. She motioned Lily to join her. The man slid a crosshatched metal gate in front of them, then cranked a heavy lever on the wall. Lily heard a loud grinding sound. She felt the floor lurch, and her stomach dropped to her knees.

"What's happening?" she cried.

"Haven't you ridden an elevator before?" Mae asked.

Lily grabbed the gate in alarm. As the booth passed a tower window, she peered out to discover Dreamland spread below her.

"There's the parade!" cried Mae.

In only seconds the elevator had climbed so high Lily could see over the park walls. Surf Avenue was still filled with marching bands and crepe-papered floats.

The tower wall blocked her view for a minute.

"Just wait till the *next* window," said Mae. "Okay"— she pointed excitedly—"look over there. You can see right into Luna!"

Across Surf Avenue was a sight Lily could hardly believe. All the times she had passed Luna Park on her way to Dreamland, she had never gone inside. Now she could see it was as big as Dreamland and filled with rides, side-shows, and a rainbow of pastel-colored minarets.

"Hey!" Mae laughed. "There's an elephant sliding down the Shoot-the-Chutes!"

Lily spotted Luna's water ride as a gray shape slid down the ramp and hit the pool. The splash sent spray high into the air.

The elevator continued to climb, and once more she

could see only the tower wall. A few seconds later the booth jolted to a halt.

"Observation deck," said the doorman, sliding open the gate. "Watch your step now."

Mae jumped out onto the balcony.

"What did I tell you!" she exclaimed, waving her hand across the scene. "You can see Manhattan!"

Lily stepped onto the balcony and gazed out. In front of her lay the tip of Coney Island and the lighthouse at Norton's Point. Beyond she could see the whole New York bay filled with boats.

"Look way up there," said Mae. "If you squint, you can see the Statue of Liberty!"

Through half-closed eyes Lily looked toward the far end of the harbor. She could just make out the shape of a human figure surrounded by water.

"I was there once," Mae boasted. "I went all the way to the crown!"

"In an elevator?" asked Lily.

"Of course not. I climbed the stairs—three hundred and fifty-four of them," said Mae.

"Someday I'm going to do that," declared Lily, a little enviously.

She rested her arms on the balcony guardrail. The sun warmed her face as she watched a large ship steam slowly up the bay.

"I wonder where that big one came from," Lily said dreamily.

"I know where it's going," said Mae. "Right to Ellis Island."

"Were you there, too?" asked Lily.

"No, my parents came before I was born," said Mae.

"Did they bring anything special with them?" Lily asked.

"Like what?"

"Like something their parents had."

"Sure," said Mae. "It's a jewelry box with velvet lining. My mother says she never let go of it the whole time they were traveling. She keeps letters in it now. You can see it sometime, if you want."

"You ladies ready to ride back down?" called the elevator man.

"We better go or we'll miss the show," Mae said.

As the car descended, Lily watched the harbor disappear and the attractions of Dreamland grow bigger. At the tower bottom, the gate slid open.

"I should get back," said Lily, looking around.

"C'mon," coaxed Mae. "We can still get good seats if we hurry."

Lion of Judah

THE LEOPARD ACT was just ending when they reached Bostock's. The two girls scrambled onto a bench near the caged arena.

"And now, what you've all been waiting for!" sang the ringmaster. "Dreamland's most fearless animal tamer. A modern-day Daniel in the Lion's Den. Bostock's is proud to present—Captain Jack Bonavita!"

A man in a smoke gray uniform sprinted into the ring and bowed deeply to the crowd. As he straightened, his whip whistled through the air. A stream of lions poured in around him, snarling and shaking their heads.

Bonavita stalked back and forth in their midst, cracking his whip to prod them onto a high set of wooden platforms. When they were settled, he walked to the center of the ring. A large hoop hung suspended from a wire overhead. The lion tamer pulled a small packet from his uniform and flicked his hand toward the hoop. The circle burst into flames.

On their benches, the lions shifted restlessly. The biggest of them lifted its huge head and roared. Lily shuddered as the sound echoed through the arena.

"That's Sultan!" cried Mae.

Lily glanced at her. A few rows ahead she noticed a man's hand hovering over a sheet of brown paper. She leaned forward to see. It was her father!

"I have to leave!" she whispered.

"What?" Mae clutched her arm. "You'll miss the best part!"

Lily looked again at the ring. Now Bonavita stood in front of Sultan's perch. He dangled his whip and the lion clambered down, edging slowly toward the flames. A few feet away it stopped and growled low in its throat. The whip hissed and the lion crouched to spring through the hoop. Suddenly it turned and reared on its hind legs, towering over Bonavita.

The audience gasped. Bonavita thrust the butt of his whip at Sultan's head, forcing it farther and farther back until the lion was standing almost straight up. Lily searched nervously for her father. He had stopped drawing, his eyes riveted on the ring.

She could not let him see her. Quickly she slid from her seat and groped her way outside, stopping just to catch her breath. She knew she should go right back to the carousel, but she couldn't, not when her mother and sister were so close. Lily turned and ran straight for the incubator clinic.

"What in the name of—!" stammered the barker blocking the door. "This is no day to be visiting!"

"I have to find her!"

She dodged past him into the glass-lined room. Her eyes swept the row of cribs. Rose's stood empty. She shrank back from the glass.

"Lily!"

She whirled around.

"Momme!"

Lily burst into tears as her mother gathered her into her arms.

"It's all right, *neshomele,* it's all right. They moved Rose to another incubator. Thank God, she's over the worst."

Lily's father rushed into the room.

"I saw her going out of Bostock's," he panted. "I thought I could catch her!"

"Bostock's? What were you doing there?" her mother demanded. "Did Golda let you go off alone?"

"She didn't know," Lily cried. "I went with that girl Mae. Her father's a policeman."

"Anything could have happened to you!" her father shouted.

"Srul, not here," her mother said sharply. "Not here. Take Lily home."

Lily's father was silent while he led her through Dreamland and out along Surf Avenue. As they neared the carousel, Lily could hear the band organ playing the Dreamland waltz.

"*Totte . . . ,*" she started, looking up at him.

"You will not go to Feltman's again after this," he said harshly, pulling her past the flashing lights.

Lily strained to look back for a glimpse of the rose horse, but the crowds were too thick. She followed her father sadly as they crossed the street and turned toward Samuel and Golda's house. When they entered the kitchen, her father set his papers heavily on the table.

Lily stood across from him, turning an angry question around and around in her mind. She took a deep breath.

"*Totte,*" she asked, "why were you at Bostock's?"

"I thought that was coming." Her father sighed. "Here, see for yourself."

He spread his drawings across the table so she could look at them. In one a leopard crouched, ready to spring. In another a lion reared on two legs, about to strike.

"I went to study the animals as they moved," he told her. "I had to know how they looked, to finish the carving for the synagogue."

Carefully he raised up the wooden piece begun the night before. Now Lily could see clearly the twin tablets of Moses in the center, inscribed with the Ten Commandments in Hebrew. Above the right tablet an eagle soared with outstretched wings. Below the left a deer leapt through a forest. The other two corners were not yet carved.

"The design comes from a saying in the *Pirke Ovos*," he said. " 'Be as strong as a leopard, swift as an eagle, fleet as a deer, and brave as a lion to serve thy father who is in heaven.' "

"Was your father a carousel carver, too?" Lily asked softly.

"Yes," said her father, laying the carving flat again. "The year we left Kishinev he was killed in a *pogrom* while the police stood by and watched. His name was Yide Leib, 'Lion of Judah.' "

Slowly he collected his sketches into a pile and set them aside. He sat motionless for several minutes, his

hand covering his eyes. Then he lifted his face and picked up a narrow chisel from the table.

"I thought of a Hebrew name for you while I was drawing," he said gently. "What do you think of *Leviah?* It means 'lioness.' "

"I like that," Lily said.

"Good. Now I need your help."

Her father cupped her palm around the chisel's handle and curled his fingers over hers. As they began to carve, Lily felt the blade cut deep into the grain.

Little Roses

THE LAST TWO WEEKS before *Shevuos,* Lily lost count of all the carousel horses she painted. On the forty-ninth day of the *omer* she was even busier helping Golda prepare for the holiday. All morning they baked *challah,* stuffed *blintzes* with soft cheese, and wove garlands of pink and yellow roses to decorate the silver Torah crowns.

"Flowers on the Torah?" Lily asked. Carefully she looped the strands of roses into a wicker handbasket.

"They remind us of the story that when God gave the Israelites the commandments, the world was filled with wonderful smells," said Golda.

"You'll come to synagogue tomorrow, too, won't you?" asked Lily. She bathed her face in the steam as Golda pulled two golden-crusted loaves from the oven.

"Of course," Golda said, "for your naming ceremony, and to stand and hear them read the Ten Commandments out loud. Your father's there now. He's hanging the new carving over the ark."

She wiped her hands on her apron. Then she reached up into a high cupboard and pulled out a sheet of white paper.

"What's that for?" asked Lily.

"Your *totte* and Samuel aren't the only ones who learned to carve in Kishinev," Golda answered mysteriously.

She smoothed the paper over a clean wooden breadboard and pressed a large, round plate on top. With a sharp knife, she traced all around the edge to cut out a paper circle. Carefully she fastened the circle to the board with tiny nails.

Lily watched as Golda cut away bit after bit of the paper, until only a web of white lines showed against the wood. Finally she removed the nails and held the circle up to the light. In the center Lily could see the perfect shape of a Torah scroll, surrounded by cutouts of birds, fish, and fruit. Above them all, a canopy of flowers arched between two pillars topped by Jewish stars.

"Where did you learn that?" Lily asked in wonder.

"When I was little, I loved watching my mother make paper-cuts to decorate the house and the synagogue for *Shevuos*," Golda said. "It always seemed like magic. She called them *reyzelech*—little roses. Sometimes she even made them to hang in a new baby's cradle, for good luck."

"Can you show me?" asked Lily.

Golda nodded. She helped Lily mix flour and water into a thin paste. As they glued the paper-cut to the kitchen window, Lily looked outside to find Mae watching them from across the street. Lily smiled. Mae waved to her, then turned and skipped away out of sight.

"You'll see her again, Lily. Don't worry," said Golda.

"I don't know how," said Lily, shaking her head.

She was washing up when her father came to take her to Dreamland, to visit Rose in the incubator one last time. Her mother met them at the clinic door.

"Today can I hold her, *Momme?*" Lily asked in front of Rose's crib.

"Tomorrow, at the synagogue," answered her mother, stroking Lily's cheek.

Lily tapped gently on the window. Her sister looked straight at her and blinked.

"What will her Hebrew name be?" she asked.

"*Rut,* for Ruth, whose story is read on *Shevuos.*"

"Then, she's coming home with us, isn't she?" said Lily. "Back to where we really live."

"Rose is coming with us, but we're not going back there," her father said. "The carousel shop will have plenty of orders this winter. Doctor Couney asked *Momme* to stay and work at the clinic till it shuts for the season in September. We've already found a place to live near Samuel and Golda's."

"But you said, when Rose came out of the incubator, we'd go home!" Lily cried. "I thought when we finished counting the *omer,* everything would go back the way it used to be!"

"Nothing can go back exactly the way it was," her mother replied, touching her father's hand. "Now this is our home."

The words echoed in Lily's ears that night as she lay on the sofa, listening to the faraway rhythm of the waves. The holiday candles, lit just before sunset, had long since burned out.

"It's almost midnight," called her father from the doorway. "You're still awake, Lily? Come on, then, you can climb up to the roof with us."

She followed him through the attic, up a ladder to the roof, where Golda and Samuel sat on an old blanket. The noise of laughter and carousel music floated up to them from Feltman's restaurant. Lily looked out toward

Dreamland, its thousands of electric lights shimmering against the darkness.

"When I was your age, Lily," said Samuel, "we used to stay up all night for *Shevuos,* to hear your grandfather lead the *tikkun,* the Torah discussion."

Lily sat down next to him on the blanket.

"I remember how he would whisper when he told about the giving of the commandments at Mount Sinai," Samuel went on. " 'All was still,' he would say. 'Not a bird sang, not an animal made a noise. Even the ocean was silent.' Then he would tell us to watch the heavens, because on *Shevuos,* he said, they would open for just one moment, and in that moment, any prayer would be answered."

Lily leaned back on her elbows and gazed up. The stars glowed like silver pins on a bolt of blue-black cloth. She stared at them for a long time, until the sounds of people and carousels faded away.

"Time to go in," her father said.

Lily stood up to see Golda and Samuel disappearing down the ladder into the house.

"Totte," she asked, helping him fold the blanket, "if we stay at Coney Island, could I still work in the carousel shop sometimes?"

"If Samuel needs help," said her father.

"And I'd go to school here, wouldn't I?"

"Of course."

"And maybe, someday, I might even ride the rose horse again."

"No, Lily," her father said. "Even if I said yes, it couldn't happen. They shipped that horse on the train, yesterday, to a park in California."

Through a blur of tears, Lily moved near the ladder to set her foot on the top rung.

"*Techterl.*" Her father stopped her. "I have something for you."

He pulled a small parcel from his pocket and gave it to her. Lily tore off the brown paper wrapping. Inside was a carved wooden figurine the size of her hand, painted exactly like the rose horse.

"Soon we'll have our own Rose with us," he said, "but I thought you would miss this one."

She reached up to him. He bent to put his arms around her. She pressed her hair against his cheek, and he held her for a long moment before they climbed down.

In the morning Lily set the rose horse on her pillow and tucked in her new white shirtwaist from the Sears, Roebuck catalogue.

"Come on, Lily," said her father, when she came into the kitchen. "*Momme* and your sister will be waiting for us."

He ushered her out the door, shutting it behind him.

"Wait, *Totte*," she said suddenly, pushing back past him to open it again.

From the kitchen table, Lily grabbed the basket full of flowers for the Torah and slid the handle over her arm.

"I almost forgot," she whispered as her fingers brushed the silken petals and she breathed in the sweet smell of roses.

GLOSSARY

For Yiddish words listed here, a final *e* is read as a separate syllable with a short vowel sound. *Ch* is pronounced like a soft clearing in the back of the throat. A number of words and names in the story are spelled according to the regional dialect that was spoken by Jews in Kishinev.

ARK—ceremonial cabinet in the synagogue, where Torah scrolls are kept for worship

BLINTZES—thin pancakes stuffed with cheese or fruit, traditionally eaten with other dairy foods on *Shevuos* (Yiddish)

DECORATION DAY—original name for Memorial Day

DI GOLDENE MEDINE—the Golden Land, popular immigrant name for America (Yiddish)

FORVERTS—*Jewish Daily Forward,* one of the most widely circulated and influential Yiddish newspapers (Yiddish)

CHALLAH—braided egg bread (Hebrew)

KISHINEV—East European city (then the capital of Bessarabia), site of a brutal *pogrom* against the Jewish population during Passover 1903. Officials falsely claimed that a Jewish carousel maker provoked the massacre. In fact, the anti-Semitic attack was planned months ahead and carried out with the help of local authorities.

K'NEHORE BENDL—"evil-eye ribbon," red ribbon used as a charm for protection against the evil eye, which according to superstition could cause illness or harm (Yiddish)

KOSHER—an observance of the Jewish laws for preparing and eating food (Hebrew)

LAG B'OMER—thirty-third day of the period between *Pesach* and *Shevuos,* commemorating the end of a plague among students of the famous Rabbi Akibah (Hebrew)

LEVIAH—lioness (Hebrew)

MIREL—Miriam, woman's name (Yiddish)

MOMME—Mama (Yiddish)

NESHOMELE—darling, or little soul (Yiddish)

OMER—seven-week period that begins the second night of Passover and leads up to *Shevuos.* "Counting the *omer*" refers to the ritual counting, as commanded in the Torah, of each of the forty-nine days. (In the time of the Temple in Jerusalem, *omer* also meant the measure of barley brought to the Temple as a spring offering.) (Hebrew)

PESACH—Passover, holiday that celebrates the escape of the Jewish people from slavery in Egypt (Hebrew)

PIRKE OVOS—Ethics of the Fathers, a collection of inspirational sayings studied in spring and summer (Hebrew)

POGROM—a government-sponsored attack against the Jewish population (Russian)

RED HOTS—hot dogs

REYZELE—little rose (Yiddish)

REYZELECH—little roses, a folk-art form of paper cutouts, used as decorations during Jewish holidays or as charms to ward off evil spirits (Yiddish)

ROMANCE SIDE—more intricately carved side of a carousel horse. On carousels carved in the United States (which turn counterclockwise), the romance side is the right side; on European carousels (which traditionally turn clockwise), the romance side is the left.

"ROZHINKES MIT MANDLEN"—"Raisins and Almonds," popular lullaby by Abraham Goldfaden, "father" of the Yiddish theater (Yiddish)

RUT—Ruth, woman's name (Hebrew)

SHEVUOS—Festival of Weeks, holiday that celebrates the Jewish people receiving the Torah, including the Ten Commandments, at Mount Sinai. *Shevuos* is also a harvest holiday (Bringing of the First Fruits), celebrated by decorating homes and synagogues with greenery and flowers. (Hebrew)

SHMIL—Samuel, man's name (Yiddish)

SPIEL—barker or salesman's talk

SONG OF SONGS—lyrical poem in the Bible, believed to have been written by King Solomon

SRUL—Israel, man's name (Yiddish)

TECHTERL—little daughter (Yiddish)

TIKKUN—all-night study of Torah portions or other religious writings, held the first night of *Shevuos* (Hebrew)

TORAH—the five books of Moses, containing the principal 613 commandments of Jewish law, including the Ten Commandments. Torahs used in the synagogue for worship are handwritten on one continuous scroll and wrapped around two wooden spindles, often topped with silver crowns. (Hebrew)

TOTTE—Papa (Yiddish)

YIDE LEIB—Lion of Judah, man's name, taken from one of the most prominent Biblical symbols of the Jewish people, symbolizing strength (Yiddish)

ZEYDE—Grandfather (Yiddish)

The illustrations in this book were done in
black Prismacolor pencil on layout paper.
The display type was set in Bellvue
by Kaelin Chappell.
The text type was set in Monotype Bulmer
by PennSet, Inc., Bloomsburg, Pennsylvania.
Printed and bound by RR Donnelley & Sons,
Harrisonburg, Virginia.
This book was printed on seventy-pound
Glatfelter Offset machine finish.
Production supervised by Warren Wallerstein
and Kent MacElwee
Designed by Kaelin Chappell